SEARCH FOR THE SUNKEN CITY

Martin Oliver

Illustrated by Brenda Haw

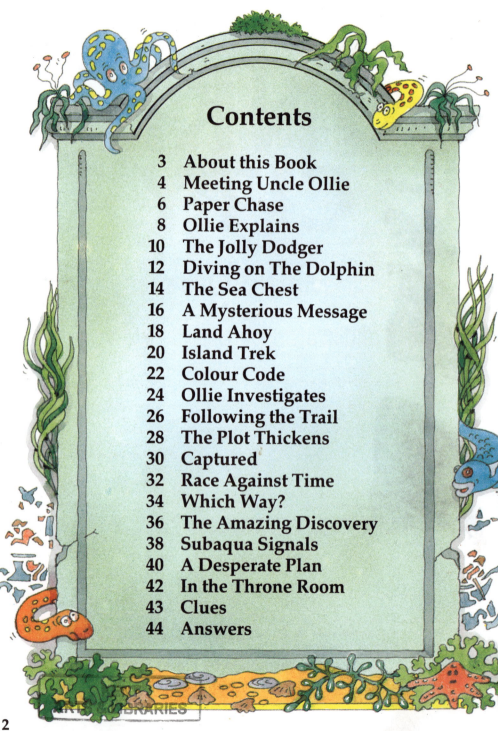

Contents

About this Book

Search for the Sunken City is an exciting story which takes you on a thrilling adventure above and below the seas.

Throughout the book, there are lots of tricky puzzles and perplexing problems which you must solve in order to understand the next part of the story.

You may need to flick back through the book to help you find an answer. There are extra clues on page 43 and you can check your answers on pages 44 to 48.

Toby and Flic's adventure began one day when the phone rang. It was Uncle Ollie, the world-famous marine archaeologist...

Hello Flic, Toby . . . Great news, I've discovered the wreck of an old galleon . . . I think it's The Dolphin which belonged to the famous explorer, San Miguel Da Silva . . . We've found some incredible things . . . Your holiday should be very exciting . . . Yes, I'll meet you on the beach as arranged.

Toby

Flic

Uncle Ollie

Meeting Uncle Ollie

Toby and Flic scrambled over the rocks to the busy beach. Flic shaded her eyes and looked around. Where was Uncle Ollie?

In the distance they heard the roar of an engine and a whoosh of spray. It was Ollie racing towards the beach in a dinghy.

Ollie jumped ashore, waving to Flic and Toby. He rushed up the beach and led them into his hut.

"Great to see you," he said, emptying out his bag. "I've got some amazing things to show you."

"They're from The Dolphin," explained Ollie, as Toby and Flic gazed at the odd collection of objects.

"Since I discovered the wreck I've been rushed off my flippers," said Ollie, taking Flic and Toby outside.

"I hope these finds will help me solve a mystery that has puzzled explorers for years," he continued.

Flic and Toby leant forward eagerly.

"Let me explain," he began, when suddenly . . .

They dashed inside. The shutters were wide open and the finds from The Dolphin were scattered over the floor.

"It must have been a strong breeze," said Toby.

But it had taken more than a strong breeze to do this. Flic was sure something was missing from the room.

What is missing?

5

Paper Chase

> Look, there he goes.

> Stop thief.

They raced outside to look for clues. Toby quickly spotted some footprints and a figure sprinting down the beach.

They set off in hot pursuit. Flic yelled out, but the villain only ran faster. Toby and Flic accelerated and began to catch up. ▶

June 9th. The storm is over but we are badly damaged and off course. Our only chance is to make for land to carry out repairs and take on fresh supplies.
June 10th. Sighted an uncharted group of islands. Dropped anchor and launched the jolly boat to explore. We first landed on a

driven away by sheer numbers. We pushed off hurriedly. I steered our boat SW between a reef to port and three jagged rocks to starboard to an island with two hillocks at its centre. We left empty-handed, headed for the black island due S. swung SE to explore a half-sunken ship, then continued SE.

Pedro. I left the ship on our island first, giving the locals

top of the yellow rock to star-board, then dive.
I sealed a chart of these islands in the sea chest bearing my crest and stowed it in my cabin aboard The Dolphin.

"Who was that?" gasped Toby, picking himself up.

"And why did he steal Da Silva's diary," asked Flic. "Maybe Ollie will know."

Ollie arrived panting and wheezing. As he struggled to get his breath back, he shook his head at their questions. Then he pointed to some scraps of paper lying on the sand.

The thief splashed into the water and jumped aboard a getaway boat. The motor immediately roared into life.

Toby made a despairing dive, but it was too late! He and Flic could only watch as the boat zoomed out to sea.

or foal shaped isle, but it was barren and the E. We found no water here seaweed. So we rowed the story isle.' As we landed on island due E. We found no water here red crabs scuttled angrily to attack. We missed some but were thousands of

We landed on the first island in our path and found fresh water, wild goats and plentiful wildfowl. We beached the Dolphin there. June 11th. The hull will take months to repair. The crew began building some huts, a windmill and a look-out post ...

Aug 20th. An incredible day!! Have made the most amazing dis-

"I saw them fall out of the thief's hand as you chased after him," he explained breathlessly. "If we can fit them together, they might help us find out what the crook was after."

Flic and Toby picked up the scraps. They were covered in old-fashioned handwriting.

What do the scraps of paper say?

Ollie Explains

Toby and Flic turned to Uncle Ollie, their heads buzzing with questions. But before they could say anything, Ollie hurried them into the dinghy.

"A chart . . . a chart in a sea chest," he muttered rereading the pieces of Da Silva's diary. "Maybe it's still there. We must search the wreck."

"Hang on a minute," Flic interrupted. "What's going on?"

Ollie smiled and handed over the tiller to Toby. As they sped away from the shore, he began to explain ....

Wherever he explored, he left a gift bearing his famous family crest.

The Captain of The Dolphin was San Miguel Da Silva, an intrepid adventurer and explorer. Da Silva sailed all over the world with his trusty crew.

Da Silva returned from his voyages with amazing tales of the strange animals and lands he had seen. The farther he travelled, the stranger his tales became, until no one believed him.

Da Silva's most incredible tale was his discovery of a fabulous sunken city. He claimed it was the mythical city of Mare Vellos.

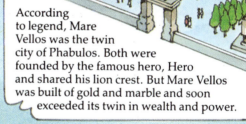

Its glory increased until, so the legend says, Mare Vellos was struck by an earthquake and submerged by a tidal wave.

According to legend, Mare Vellos was the twin city of Phabulos. Both were founded by the famous hero, Hero and shared his lion crest. But Mare Vellos was built of gold and marble and soon exceeded its twin in wealth and power.

When no one believed his tale, Da Silva set sail to bring back proof of the city but he never returned. The Dolphin was caught in a storm and sank without trace.

Any proof Da Silva raised was lost with him. Since then many people have searched for the city, but in vain. The ruins of Phabulos were found years ago, but Da Silva's story of his discovery has been discounted as a hoax until now . . .

The Jolly Dodger

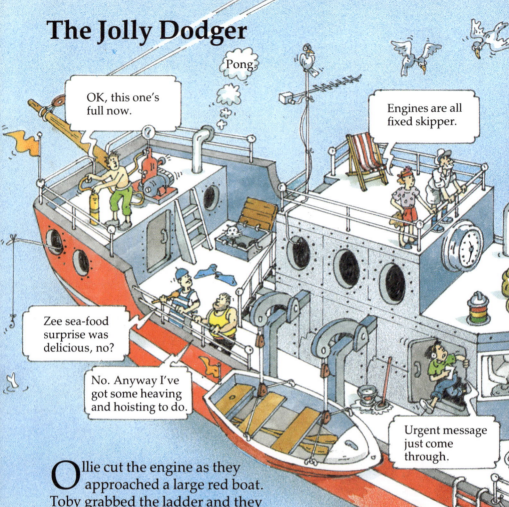

O llie cut the engine as they approached a large red boat. Toby grabbed the ladder and they all scrambled aboard.

"I hired everything myself," Ollie stated proudly, as Toby and Flic stared round at the ramshackle diving gear and the motley crew.

"Time to get kitted up for diving," said Ollie, excitedly. "But only one of you can come down with me. We're short of air and one experienced diver."

Toby and Flic looked glumly at each other. They both wanted to explore the wreck. Flic peered over Ollie's shoulder at the papers in his dive file.

As she listened to the crew, she realized that she and Toby could both dive and she knew who with.

Who can they dive with?
What about the air cylinders?

Diving on The Dolphin

Flic held onto her facemask and stepped off the ladder. Air bubbles whooshed and burst over her. She quickly ran through her equipment checks, trying to remember her diving lessons.

Then she slowly swam down to join the others. They finned over a mudbank and through a shoal of silvery fish. Toby brushed his way through a patch of sinewy seaweeds and suddenly breathed out a long stream of bubbles. Ahead lay The Dolphin.

The ship was broken in two and covered in floating fronds and barnacles. Michelle led the search and began to explore the hull. Toby peered around and out of the corner of his eye, he spotted it . . . The very thing they were looking for!

What has Toby seen?

The Sea Chest

Ollie noted the position of the chest on his site plan while the others attached a buoy to it. The four divers swam to the surface while the chest floated gently upwards.

They bobbed up and down in the swell then scrambled onto the deck of The Jolly Dodger. Toby took off his mask and watched excitedly as the chest was hoisted aboard.

It was Da Silva's chest. But did it contain his chart? Ollie picked the lock with his trusty skeleton key and tugged at the lid. Nothing happened.

It was jammed shut. Ollie tried again, this time with Flic's help. They pushed and pulled until suddenly the lid sprang open, sending them flying.

Toby stared into the chest half expecting to find it packed with ancient treasure. But the chest was empty, except for a musty smell and a roll of paper. Ollie studied it carefully. It was Da Silva's chart.

"These are the Sardonic islands, only two days' sail from here," he exclaimed. "Our next move towards the city, is to work out where Da Silva set up his base."

Where was Da Silva's island base?

A Mysterious Message

Two days later, Toby and Flic were taking first watch with Uncle Ollie. Dawn was breaking and the crew were asleep.

"Keep your eyes peeled," Ollie said. "You should see the island at any minute."

Toby and Flic scanned the horizon. Suddenly Toby's ears pricked up as he heard a whirr and a crackle of static from the radio room.

"No one should be using the radio at this time," he said. "Come on, let's investigate."

Toby motioned to Flic to follow him and tiptoed towards the radio room trying hard not to make a sound.

CLANG. He stepped on a bar of soap, skidded along the deck and crashed into a bucket and mop.

As Flic helped him to his feet, Toby thought he caught a glimpse of a shadowy figure sprinting towards the crew's quarters.

But before he could speak, Flic put her finger to her mouth and pointed to the radio room. The door was ajar and a light was shining under it.

They pulled the door open and cautiously peered in. The room was empty, but the radio was switched on and set to receive. Who had been using it? And what message had they received?

Flic noticed that the top sheet of the radio operator's pad had been hurriedly torn off.

This gave Toby an idea. Whoever received the message must have written it down on the pad. He picked up a pencil and scribbled on the top sheet of the pad. The imprint of a message appeared, but it was in code.

Can you work out what the message says?

Land Ahoy

Just then, Ollie's cry of "Land Ahoy!" echoed around The Jolly Dodger. Toby and Flic raced up to the bridge and spotted their destination – Da Silva's island dead ahead.

Instructions rang out and there was a mad scramble as the crew raced about the decks. They loaded up a strange assortment of small boats and headed towards the island.

Ollie scrambled into a boat with Toby and Flic. As he rowed for shore, Flic told him about the coded message. Who had sent it? Was the same person behind the theft of the diary?

This enemy wanted to stop them searching a place on the island. He had described it with a cryptic clue, but where was it?

Where is the place?

Island Trek

A s the trio waded ashore, Ollie thought about the crew who were busy setting up camp. One of them must be a spy, but he didn't know who.

Now was their chance to head for the windmill before the spy noticed they were gone. They hurried along a dusty track and scrambled up a steep slope.

The beach was soon left far behind as they raced on into the unknown. They hiked uphill between sharp rocks and prickly bushes. Flic turned a corner...

She gasped. They were standing in an arena. Their path to the windmill was blocked by a large semi-circular amphitheatre looming up in front of them.

Rows of seats were chiselled into the steep cliff. Some had crumbled away completely, leaving sheer rock. There was no way round.

"We'll have to go back," Ollie groaned. "Unless we can find a way up one step at a time."

Can you find a way to the top?

Colour Code

At last they reached the windmill. Toby shivered in spite of the heat. He had the spooky feeling that they were being watched. Ollie glanced at a crumbly wall. His eyes opened wide and he began scrabbling through his rucksack.

"It's incredible," he shouted, pulling out his magnifying glass. "I've found Da Silva's message."

Toby crouched beside Ollie and they stared at a section of the wall. They could clearly make out some words that were chiselled into the stone. Ollie and Toby read them aloud, but they didn't seem to make any sense.

"I'm sure that this is the key to decoding Da Silva's message," said Flic, "Now all we've got to do is find it."

When A becomes M and Z becomes L, my message I will tell. Da Silva.

Start on red, read clockwise, then stop on green and my message will be seen.

22

The trio split up and began searching the area. They checked inside the windmill, behind columns and even under the stones on the ground, but they found nothing. Ollie slumped down glumly. The trail had run dry.

Just then a sudden gust of wind whistled around the mill. The sails creaked into life, Toby glanced up and spotted words painted onto them.

What does the message say?

Ollie Investigates

Toby groaned at the thought of more clues while Flic scratched her head and stared at the message again. There was something rather odd about it, but Ollie didn't seem to mind.

"I'll look for the clues while you recheck the map and diary fragments," he said, handing them over. "Stay here and wait for me. This won't take long."

Toby and Flic glanced at the chart, but it was too hot. They flopped down in the cool shade and began to snooze.

Meanwhile Ollie scrabbled in the ruins. He brushed away some dust and peered intently at the mosaic he had uncovered.

Toby woke up with a start, feeling very thirsty. He was just about to take a swig from his water bottle when he felt something tickling his leg. He looked down and yelled.

Ollie was still looking for clues when he spotted a marble head. It was Hero, the founder of Mare Vellos. He gently pulled the head out of the wall. Then everything went black…

Toby and Flic were brushing off ants when they heard a crash and a muffled shout. Had something happened to Ollie? They picked up their bags and dashed towards the ruins.

Suddenly Flic stopped dead in her tracks. She saw something that she recognized. Ollie was in trouble!

What has Flic spotted?

Following the Trail

Toby and Flic looked at each other in horror. Where was Ollie? They followed the trail of footprints to the edge of a cliff and looked over. The footprints continued down an almost sheer rock face.

"Let's go," gulped Toby, trying hard not to look down.

They slipped and slid down the steep slope, dodging past spiky thistles and through a swarm of buzzing hornets. Flic skidded to a halt as a scorpion scuttled across their path. Toby tripped, sending an avalanche of stones rattling down. But at last they reached the bottom in one piece.

Toby stared across the bay and ducked for cover when he saw what Flic was pointing at.

THE DIRTY SWAB

Uncle Ollie! He was being hauled onto a yacht by a tough-looking villain.

"We must get aboard that boat and find out what's going on," said Flic.

How? They would be spotted if they tried to swim across the bay, but they could reach the cliff top behind the boat unnoticed.

How can they get aboard the boat?

The Plot Thickens

"Where is the map and the rest of the diary?"

"It's no good Schwindler. I'll never tell you where they are. You'll never find the city."

Toby and Flic leapt from rock to rock and clambered silently onto the deck of the boat. They crept past a snoozing sentry and peered in through a porthole.

"That must be the dastardly crook behind all this," gasped Flic, staring at the tall figure threatening Ollie.

"His name is Dr Schwindler," said Toby, pointing to the passport that was among some papers lying on the table below.

He carefully studied the photos and sheets of paper. Now it was clear why Schwindler was so interested in finding Da Silva's sunken city.

Name: Dr Schwindler

Occupation: Dealer in ancient treasures

Distinguishing features; loud ties and monocle.

Plans for looting sunken city

Estimated value of treasure in city – $15,000,000

Estimated cost of recovering treasure – $1,000,000

PROFIT = $14,000,000

There was a knock on the cabin door. Schwindler hurriedly picked up his plans and locked them in a drawer, uncovering some pieces of Da Silva's diary.

Toby and Flic gasped as a familiar figure walked into the cabin . . . Michelle Silver! She was the spy amongst their crew.

Schwindler turned back to Ollie and tried to force him to reveal the location of the city.

"I know where it is," Toby whispered, reading Schwindler's pieces of the diary. "But first we must rescue Ollie."

Where should they dive?

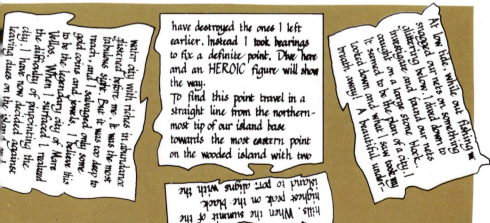

Captured

S chwindler realized he was getting nowhere with Ollie, and he stormed out of the cabin with Michelle. As soon as the crooks had gone, Toby squirmed and squeezed his way through the porthole. He landed in the cabin with a thud.

They all held their breath. The boat was quiet. No one had heard. Flic wriggled in and dashed over to Ollie.

"Am I glad to see you," Ollie whispered, as Flic wrestled with the knots tying him to the wall. "We must get out of here and stop those villains."

The last rope fell to the ground. Ollie stretched his arms and legs, but Flic froze. Footsteps pounded towards them. They rushed to the porthole, desperate to escape. But it was too late.

The cabin door swung open and they came face to face with the sneering Dr Schwindler and his henchmen.

"Welcome aboard," he hissed. "There will be no way out for you three now."

Before I discover the city, I will pay a visit to your ship.

The evil doctor ordered his sidekick to tie up the trio, then he tipped out their bags. He spotted the map and fragments and grabbed them triumphantly.

"Hah! Now the sunken city is mine," he cackled. "Don't try to escape. Michelle will guard you very closely while I 'research' the treasury."

Schwindler and his crooked crony slammed the door shut. Toby's brain jolted into action. They had to escape and foil Schwindler's plan. But how? If only Michelle wasn't convinced that they were looters.

Suddenly Toby realized there was evidence to prove that Schwindler was the real looter. If only they could get it.

What is the proof?
How can they get it?

Race Against Time

Michelle read Schwindler's plans and needed no more convincing. She quickly untied the others, led them off the deserted boat and into the dinghy.

They soon reached The Jolly Dodger and jumped aboard. The race against Schwindler was on. Michelle started the engines. Following Da Silva's directions, Toby and Flic looked out for the yellow rock and the black peak while Ollie steered a straight course to the dive spot.

If we run into trouble or find anything down there, I will let off this signal flare. Lower your strongest steel net where you see it.

They kitted up in record time and Michelle, Ollie and Toby dived into the sea. Flic scanned the horizon for a sign of Schwindler. She reached for an underwater signal flare and whispered a plan to the captain.

She climbed down the ladder and was about to jump in, when Michelle shot out of the water.

"There's a limpet mine attached to the hull," she spluttered. "And it's timed to go off in four minutes."

"Schwindler designed it," she shouted. "The numbers in each row, column and diagonal add up to 34. The buttons are numbered 1 to 16, but some numbers have rusted away. To defuse the bomb, we must press button number 13. But we have to find it first."

They dived down to the others who were tugging at the bomb. Flic's mind whirred into action as she glanced at the clock. She gulped. Time was running out.

Which button should they press?

Which Way?

Michelle defused the bomb with seconds to spare. It was a narrow escape, but now they must get back to the search for the sunken city.

Ollie led the way as they swam down through the shallow water. Weeds floated in the current and eels darted out of crevices in the jagged coral reefs.

Suddenly Michelle spotted a round object lying on the sea bed. She picked it up and gasped. It was a man's head. Then she realized that it was part of a marble statue.

Ollie finned over to her and stared at the find. He recognized the face as Hero and noticed the base of the statue firmly embedded in the sea floor. With a flash of inspiration he realized what Da Silva's clue "an HEROIC figure will point the way" meant. He signalled to the others to begin looking for more pieces.

If they could rebuild the statue of Hero, it would point towards the city.

In which direction should they swim?

The Amazing Discovery

They swam in the direction the statue pointed. Suddenly the sea bed fell away beneath them. All four let out a gasp of air bubbles. Shimmering below were the ruins of an ancient city. There were great buildings made of marble blocks and glistening columns. They had found the sunken city. Toby turned a subaqua somersault, but there was no time to celebrate.

First they had to stop Schwindler. They knew that he was heading for the treasury, but where was it? Ollie quickly found the stone plan of the city mentioned by Da Silva. He brushed away the weeds and studied the writing. He soon found the treasury on the plan and pointed it out.

Which building is the treasury?

Subaqua Signals

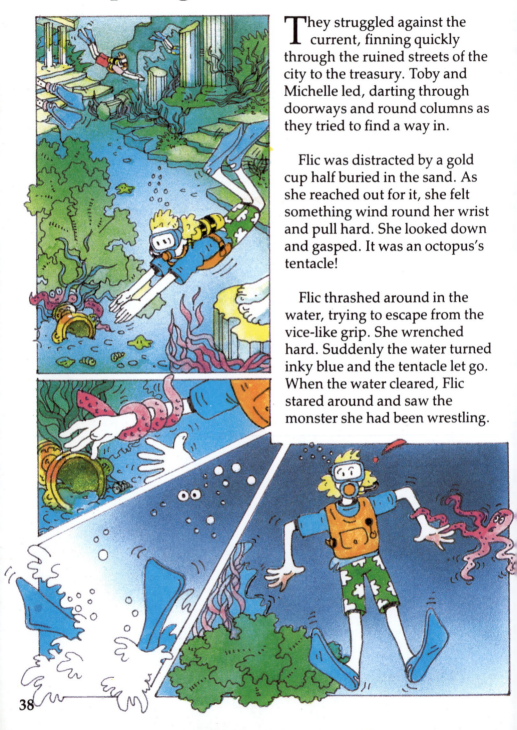

They struggled against the current, finning quickly through the ruined streets of the city to the treasury. Toby and Michelle led, darting through doorways and round columns as they tried to find a way in.

Flic was distracted by a gold cup half buried in the sand. As she reached out for it, she felt something wind round her wrist and pull hard. She looked down and gasped. It was an octopus's tentacle!

Flic thrashed around in the water, trying to escape from the vice-like grip. She wrenched hard. Suddenly the water turned inky blue and the tentacle let go. When the water cleared, Flic stared around and saw the monster she had been wrestling.

Feeling rather silly, she paddled through a marble arch to join the others. As they swam round to the front of the treasury, an electric eel curved past, almost touching Uncle Ollie.

Toby felt a hand grab his arm. Michelle pointed to Ollie who was waving his hands wildly at them. Why? Perhaps he was in trouble? Had he been shocked by the eel?

All of a sudden Toby realized what Ollie was doing. He was using his underwater sign language. But what was he trying to say? Ollie repeated his signals slowly.

What is Uncle Ollie saying?

A Desperate Plan

The trio spotted the danger immediately. Cruising through the submerged city was a mini-submarine . . . with Schwindler at the helm.

At that moment the evil crook saw the divers. He snarled with anger and turned the mini-sub towards them. There was only one thing to do – swim for it.

They finned through the city, with Schwindler hard on their flippers. Flic glanced up and spotted a reef with a coral arch ahead. A desperate plan formed in her brain.

She signalled to the others and they swerved through the coral arch, closely followed by Schwindler. There was a nerve-jangling screech. The mini-sub was stuck fast.

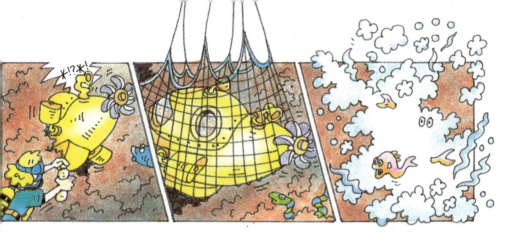

Flic moved quickly. As Schwindler tried to back out of trouble, Flic let off the signal flare.

The Jolly Dodger lowered a steel net. Schwindler reversed out of the arch and into the trap.

He released the ballast to try to escape and the water frothed with bubbles and seaweed.

When the water cleared, Ollie, Toby, Flic and Michelle watched as the helpless villain and his crew were hauled out of the water to be clapped in irons.

Flic looked over to check her oxygen and spotted something that hadn't been visible before.

What has Flic noticed?

In the Throne Room

The four divers made their way through the clear water to explore the weed-covered building. They swam through the entrance and gasped at the magnificent room before them. They were inside the actual throne room of the sunken city.

Ollie was sure that the city was Mare Vellos, but he needed proof. And what about Da Silva? Had he really discovered it all those years ago? Suddenly Ollie spotted what he was looking for.

What has Ollie seen?

Clues

Pages 4-5

This is easy. Use your eyes.

Pages 6-7

Trace over the fragments of paper. Then piece them together.

Pages 10-11

Look carefully at Ollie's crew list. What are the crew saying?

Pages 12-13

You can see Da Silva's crest on page 8.

Pages 14-15

Port is left. Starboard is right.

Pages 16-17

Try thinking backwards.

Pages 18-19

First think of a word for a legal document about your last wishes. Then change the order of the letters in the word "mind" and put them into the middle of the word for a legal document.

Pages 20-21

They can jump over the gaps between rows of seats.

Pages 22-23

Write out the alphabet then substitute M for A, N for B, O for C and so on until A is substituted for O and finally L is substituted for Z.

Pages 24-25

Look carefully at what is on the ground.

Pages 26-27

Watch out for creepers with snakes on them.

Pages 28-29

Piece these fragments together with those on pages 6 and 7. Then check the map on page 15.

Pages 30-31

Where are Schwindler's plans?

Pages 32-33

Add up each column in turn. No number is repeated.

Pages 34-35

This is easy. Find all the pieces of the statue and put them together.

Pages 36-37

Compare the shape of the buildings in the city with the plan.

Pages 38-39

Check Ollie's underwater signals on page 11.

Pages 40-41

Keep your eyes peeled.

Page 42

Look back to pages 8 and 9.

Answers

Pages 4-5

This document is now missing from the room.

Pages 6-7

This is the document when pieced together. It is not complete because the thief has stolen the rest of the fragments.

June 9th. The storm is over but we are badly damaged and off course. Our only chance is to make for land to carry out repairs and take on fresh supplies.
June 10th. Sighted an uncharted group of islands. Dropped anchor and launched the jolly boat to explore. We first landed on a

skull-shaped isle, but it was barren of food and water so we rowed SE to a thickly wooded flat island. We found no water here and continued past foul-smelling seaweed to port towards an island due E. As we landed on the stony isle, thousands of red crabs scuttled angrily to attack. We roasted some but were

driven away by sheer numbers. We pushed off hurriedly. I steered our boat SW between a reef to port and three jagged rocks to starboard to an island with two hillocks at its centre. We left empty-handed, headed for the black island due S. swung SE to explore a half-sunken ship, then continued SE.

We landed on the first island in our path and found fresh water, wild goats and plentiful wildfowl. We beached the Dolphin there. June 11th. The hull will take months to repair. The crew began building some huts, a windmill and a look-out post ...
Aug 20th. An incredible day!! Have made the most amazing dis-

covery. I left clues giving the location of the find on our island base.

The stolen diary fragments go here.

top of the yellow rock to star-board, then dive.
I sealed a chart of these islands in the sea chest bearing my crest and stowed it in my cabin aboard The Dolphin.

Pages 10-11

They can dive with Michelle Silver, the engineer. She is the only other experienced diver in the crew who can dive that day.

Ollie's dive details say that they each need one cylinder of air per dive. You can see the four full air cylinders ringed in the picture.

Pages 12-13

Toby has spotted the sea chest with Da Silva's crest.

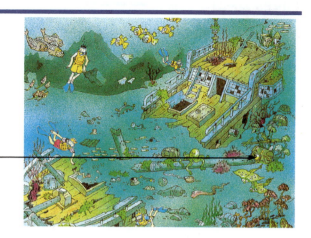

Da Silva's sea chest ——————————————

Pages 14-15

Da Silva's route to his island base is described in the diary. It is marked here in black.

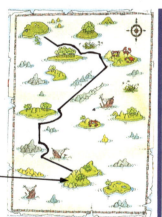

This was Da Silva's island base. ——————

Pages 16-17

The message is written backwards with wrong spacings between words. This is what it says with punctuation added:

Oliver and the two brats must not, repeat not, search at the place where "a legal document about twisted mind is driven by natural forces". Otherwise they will find a vital message and clues hidden by Da Silva.

Pages 18-19

The place on the island is described with the cryptic clue: a place where "a legal document about twisted mind is driven by natural forces". Cryptic clues can be broken down into several parts which must be solved in turn. Words used in cryptic clues have their own special meaning. This cryptic clue is solved as follows:

1. A word meaning "a legal document" is **will**.

2. "About" is an instruction to place the word **will** around the solution to the next part of the clue.
3. "Twisted mind" is an instruction to change the order of the letters in the word **mind**.
4. To solve the clue, break the word **will** and put it on either side of the mixed up letters in the word **mind**. This produces the word **windmill**. This is a place "driven by natural forces".

Pages 20-21

The route up to the top
of the amphitheatre is
marked in black.

Pages 22-23

To decode the letters on the windmill
sails write out the alphabet then
substitute M for A, N for B, O for C,
P for D, and so on through every
letter of the alphabet.

To read the message, begin decoding
the letters on the red sail, move
round clockwise, then stop on the
green sail. The rest is nonsense.

This is what the message says:

In the ruins out of sight of the
windmill I left more clues to the
location of the sunken city.

Pages 24-25

Flic has spotted a set of footprints on
the ground that are identical to the
thief's footprints on pages 6 and 7.

Flic has also spotted Ollie's
magnifying glass.

Pages 26-27

They can tie one of the creepers to
the rocks here.

Then they can climb down to these
steps.

The rest of the route onto the boat is
marked in black.

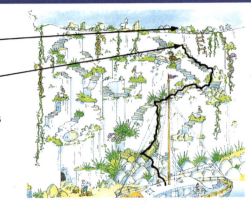

Pages 28-29

The rest of the diary fragments (stolen by the thief on page 5) complete Da Silva's directions pinpointing the location of the sunken city.

To find out where to dive for the city, draw a straight line between the landmarks mentioned. The point where the two lines cross is where they should dive for the city.

have destroyed the ones I left earlier. Instead I took bearings to fix a definite point. Dive here and an HEROIC figure will show the way.
To find this point travel in a straight line from the northern-most tip of our island base towards the most eastern point on the wooded island with two

hills. When the summit of the highest peak on the black island to port aligns with the top of the yellow rock to star-board, then dive.
I sealed a chart of these islands in the sea chest bearing my crest and stowed it in my cabin aboard The Dolphin.

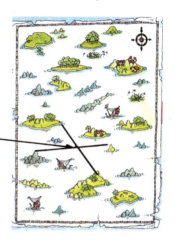

Dive here for the sunken city.

This fragment is in Toby and Flic's possession.

Pages 30-31

Schwindler's plans, which Toby saw through the porthole on page 28, prove that Schwindler intends to loot the city to make money for himself. He locked the plans in a drawer on page 29, but left the key in the cabin. To find the proof they must unlock the drawer.

The key

Pages 32-33

This is the limpet mine with all the buttons numbered correctly. To defuse the bomb they must press button number 13.

This is the intact statue.

When rebuilt, the statue points in the direction arrowed.

This building is the treasury.

You can see Ollie's signal chart on page 11. This is what he is saying.

Stop

Look

Left

Danger

Follow me

Flic has seen this building through the weeds.

Ollie has spotted two things.

The crest on the throne is Hero's lion crest. You can see this on page 9. Mare Vellos shared the crest with Phabulos. This proves that the sunken city is Mare Vellos.

The telescope with Da Silva's crest proves that Da Silva must have discovered the city.